Lexile: _____

Quiz #
154963

AR/BL: _____4.5_____

AR Points: _____1.0_____

High Risk
published in 2007 by
Hardie Grant Egmont
85 High Street
Prahran, Victoria 3181, Australia
www.hardiegrantegmont.com.au

Hardie Grant Egmont uses
Greenhouse Friendly™
ENVI Carbon Neutral Paper

GREENHOUSE FRIENDLY

CONSUMER

ENVI Carbon Neutral Paper is an Australian Government
certified Greenhouse Friendly™ Product.

The text for this book has been printed on ENVI Carbon Neutral Paper.

A CiP record for this title is available from the National Library of Australia

Text copyright © 2007 H.I. Larry
Illustration and design copyright © 2007 Hardie Grant Egmont

Cover and illustrations by Andy Hook
Based on original illustrations and design by Ash Oswald
Typeset by Pauline Haas

Printed in Australia by McPherson's Printing Group

11 13 15 14 12

TOP SECRET CODE:
HIDDEN KINGDOM

ZAC POWER

| 24 HOURS TO SAVE THE WORLD ... AND VISIT HIS GRANNY |

HIGH RISK

BY H. I. LARRY

ILLUSTRATIONS BY ANDY HOOK

hardie grant EGMONT

CHAPTER... ...ONE

What do mountain climbers do about hat-hair? Zac Power wondered, as he adjusted his woollen beanie.

It was Book Week at Zac's school, and everyone had to dress up as their favourite character from a book. Kids were dressed as giant peaches, robots, boy wizards — there was even a walking football!

The costume parade was always good for a chuckle.

Zac was dressed as a mountaineer. His favourite book was about Edmund Hillary, the first explorer to climb Mount Everest. Zac's grandpa, Agent High Pants, had read the story to him when he was little.

Zac's grandpa was the Power family's first Government Investigation Bureau (GIB) spy. Now Zac, his parents and even his brother were all GIB secret agents.

Zac sighed, thinking about how his friends would freak if they knew the cool GIB stuff he'd done. But it was top secret!

As Principal De Souza babbled on about *her* favourite book when she was a child, Zac saw a flashing red light coming from the bushes near the car park.

No-one else seemed to notice the light blinking on and off in long and short flashes.

Zac's brain switched into code-breaking mode – it was Morse code! Thanks to a GIB training course he'd done, Zac quickly realised the light was spelling out 'Z-A-C'.

Checking that no-one was looking, Zac sneaked around the bushes into the car park.

Zac saw that the red flashes were coming from the top of a large, grey rock buried in the grass near the edge of the car park.

3D rock
hologram
projection

Weird! thought Zac. *I've never seen that big rock there before . . .*

Zac bent down to touch the rock. But instead of touching a rough surface, his fingers slipped right through. The rock was a 3D hologram projection!

Red lasers scanned Zac's fingerprints. The rock shimmered, and winked off.

It must be programmed to recognise my fingerprints, thought Zac.

The 3D rock image had been hiding a low, sleek car – with a rocket engine!

The windscreen opened with a hiss. Inside, Zac saw a leather seat, a tiny chrome steering wheel, and lots of LCD displays on the dashboard. On the seat was a disk.

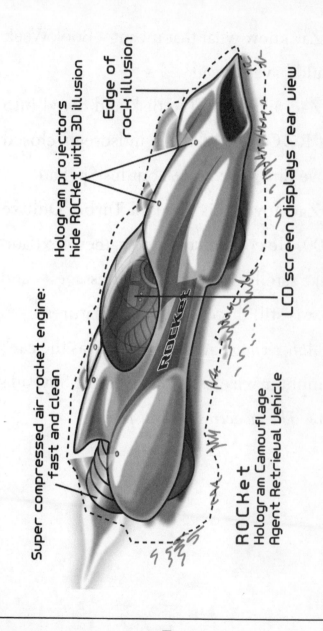

Edge of
rock illusion

Hologram projectors
hide ROCKet with 3D illusion

LCD screen displays rear view

Super compressed air rocket engine:
fast and clean

ROCKet
Hologram Camouflage
Agent Retrieval Vehicle

Zac knew what that meant – Book Week would have to wait!

Zac picked up the disk and dived into the ROCKet. As the windscreen closed above him, Zac pulled out his SpyPad.

Zac loved his SpyPad Turbo Deluxe 3000. He could play video games, text and make satellite calls, decode messages – and he was still discovering new features!

Ahh, technology, thought Zac, as the car's computer wirelessly received the SpyPad's data. *The modern spy's best friend.*

CHAPTER... ...TWO

Zac needed to get out of the school car park, and quickly! He didn't want to be seen by any kids or teachers.

A flashing red target lit up on the car's curved windscreen, showing the direction and distance to something called the Mobile Technology Lab (MTL).

First though, Zac had to read his mission. He slotted the disk into his SpyPad.

▰▰▰▰▰▰▰

CLASSIFIED
FOR THE EYES OF ZAC POWER ONLY

MESSAGE INITIATED 9:00AM

GIB has received a top-secret distress
call from our GIB agent in the
Hidden Kingdom. The country's prince
has been kidnapped!

There's only 24 hours until the Prince must
be crowned king at a special ceremony.

YOUR MISSION

- Drive to the MTL for briefing.
- Travel to the Hidden Kingdom,
and meet with local GIB agent.
- Rescue the Prince, and return him to
the Golden Palace for the crowning ceremony.

MISSION TIME REMAINING:
23 HOURS 14 MINS
END

BOOK WEEK
>>> OFF

Zac had heard about Leon's new laboratory, but he hadn't seen it. The display on the windscreen showed it was 99.8 kilometres away . . . and moving!

Excellent, Leon will have more briefing info and new gadgets for me, thought Zac, as he turned the ignition key. *Time to ROCKet!*

Zac was thrown back into his seat as the ROCKet blasted out of the car park. **VvvrrrrrrOOOOOOMMMM!!!** The ground-hugging car roared out of the school and onto the road. Zac watched his school shrink rapidly in the rear vision mirror. No-one had seen him leave.

Following the directions to the MTL, Zac was soon hurtling along the freeway.

The ROCKet could *really* fly!

Being a spy does have its rewards, thought Zac, passing cars as if they were standing still. The ROCKet was so low and fast, the other cars could barely see him!

Zac hadn't bothered to read the *Braking and Emergency Stopping* instructions, so he had to do some wild steering as he zig-zagged through the traffic at top speed.

Suddenly, the MTL target moved to the left of the windscreen display.

A moving target wasn't easy to catch, and traffic blocked the left lane. Zac needed to take the next exit — now!

He swerved onto the grass next to the freeway, and took the ROCKet under a wire fence and across a paddock. He tried a few skids in the long grass before cutting back onto a road.

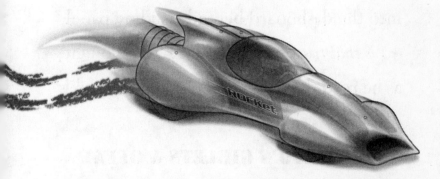

He floored it. The ROCKet ate up the distance to the MTL. Within half an hour, Zac was only two kilometres away.

How will I know which vehicle is the MTL? Zac wondered, as he got closer and closer to the flashing red target on his screen.

Then he saw the target lock on to the back of a large truck driving ahead.

The red light on his screen turned green. The steering wheel pulled itself out of Zac's grip and, with a click, contracted into the dashboard behind a sliding panel.

Is that truck really the MTL? Zac thought, as he read the name painted on the truck's doors:

GIBRALTO'S GIBLETS & OFFAL

A ramp lowered from the truck's underside, and the ROCKet drove itself up the ramp. Zac opened the ROCKet's hatch and climbed out. The truck's walls were lined with racks of disgusting offal!

Zac was met by a smiling young man in overalls. He had a crooked moustache.

Zac read the moustache-man's badge.

Hi! I'm Gino Gibralto!

Gino offered Zac a tray of shiny guts.

'Err, maybe later, thanks,' said Zac, studying Gino's face.

It didn't take Zac long to figure out that Gino was really his nerdy big brother, in a really lame disguise – Leon loved dress-ups!

Zac decided to play along. Leon *was* doing his best, after all. Thankfully Leon was now in charge of GIB technology, and was no longer a field agent like Zac.

But Leon couldn't keep up his act any longer. 'Zac,' he said, tearing off his moustache. 'Ouch! It's ME, Leon!'

'Wow . . . great disguise!' Zac said, trying not to laugh.

Leon grinned proudly, and pushed a kidney-shaped button on the wall behind him. The steel racks of organs and offal folded into the ceiling, revealing computer gear, tools and loads of spy gadgets.

'Don't worry,' Leon whispered, 'the guts are made of tofu!'

'Very, er . . . clever,' said Zac, picking up a pair of gloves with long metal claws. They looked dangerous. 'So what are these babies for?' he asked.

CHAPTER... ...THREE

Leon put his guts-platter down, squinting as he focused his geeky brain on Zac's mission. With his hands behind his back, Leon began pacing about and clearing his throat.

Zac groaned quietly – he recognised the warning signs. Leon was heading for an N.I.O. (Nerdy Information Overload)! Leon would try to tell Zac *everything* about his mission – the destination, the gadgets ...

and Zac would *still* be here 24 hours later. The key was to push Leon along so he couldn't bury you in facts.

'To answer your question,' Leon began, 'those gloves are Ice Claws – for *serious* mountain-climbing.'

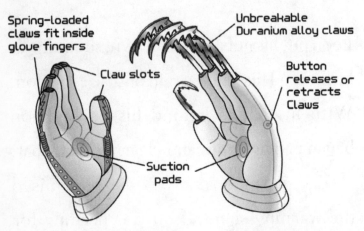

Spring-loaded claws fit inside glove fingers

Claw slots

Unbreakable Duranium alloy claws

Button releases or retracts Claws

Suction pads

Ice Claws – Extreme Ice-Climbing Gloves

'Now,' Leon said, clearing his throat again. 'You already know the Prince of the

Hidden Kingdom has disappeared. He was supposed to be crowned king tomorrow at 7pm – that's 9am tomorrow our time. He has been kidnapped.'

'Can't they put off the ceremony until we find the Prince?' Zac asked.

'Ahh, no!' Leon answered smugly. 'You see, the Hidden Kingdom follows ancient laws. A new king can *only* be crowned on the *second* full moon in the month of the harvest. According to my calculations . . .' Leon paused to do the complicated maths problem in his head.

'Basically, it *has* to be tomorrow?' Zac said quickly, wanting to get to the point.

'Yes! Or else it will be a *disaster!* A

political, economic disaster that – '

'Refresh my memory,' Zac interrupted, as he spun Leon's globe of the world. 'Where exactly *is* this country again?' Geography wasn't Zac's best subject.

Leon sighed, stopped the globe spinning, and pointed to a ring of sharp, white peaks high in the northern hemisphere. Zac could just make out a tiny green country.

Leon got back to his pacing and throat clearing. He loved a mission briefing!

'The Hidden Kingdom is in a deep, bowl-shaped valley. It is protected by a wall of mountains. Life there has not changed for centuries. No modern technology is used in the Kingdom. No cars are allowed.

No engines. In fact, no electronic devices are permitted there *at all*.'

Leon turned to look at Zac, who had been flicking through his SpyPad emails. He had one from his dad, saying they were having dinner at granny's when he got back.

'Did you hear that, Zac?' said Leon. 'NO ELECTRONIC DEVICES!'

Leon's words set off alarms for Zac. *No iPod? No SpyPad? No high-tech gadgets?*

'But Leon, in this *emergency*, we can use GIB technology, right?' Zac was suddenly feeling less confident about the mission.

Leon looked serious. 'No Zac, you *must* respect the Kingdom's laws. Anyway, I have been working on some HK-approved gadgets. This super-warm climbing suit is made of spider silk and –'

Leon stopped suddenly and looked Zac up and down. 'Err, Zac, why are you *already* wearing climbing gear?'

'Long story,' Zac sighed, and started swapping his Book Week costume for the snow-white camouflage climbing suit.

'Once you enter the Kingdom,' Leon continued, 'we cannot communicate with you. We've organised for you to connect in mid-air with our local GIB agent, code name Ringo. All the details are in your mission notes. Then, rescue the Prince!'

Zac was just about to ask about that 'mid-air' part when the MTL braked.

'Ah, we must be at the GIB airfield! Your jet is waiting,' said Leon. 'But lastly . . .'

Leon pulled a beautiful old wristwatch from his pocket and handed it to Zac.

'This belonged to Agent High Pants — grandpa. It's his original spy chronometer. It was found near where he disappeared on that jungle mission, all those years ago. I know grandpa would have loved you to have it. It's mechanical, not electronic, so it's HK-approved. I've set it to HK local time.'

SPY CHRONOMETER
TIME: 8:31 PM & 15 SECONDS
MISSION TIME LEFT:
22 HOURS,
28 MINUTES
AND 45 SECONDS

Zac examined the old watch. He turned it over and saw that some words were engraved on the back.

Feeling scared?
Make a plan instead!

That was pure grandpa! Stay positive, never give up! Once again, Zac vowed that one day he would find out what happened to his grandpa.

'Thanks, Leon,' said Zac, slipping on the watch and grabbing his backpack.

Zac jumped out of the truck and onto the runway. Up ahead he could see his ride to the Hidden Kingdom – the SuperSonic Boomerang, or SSB. It looked awesome!

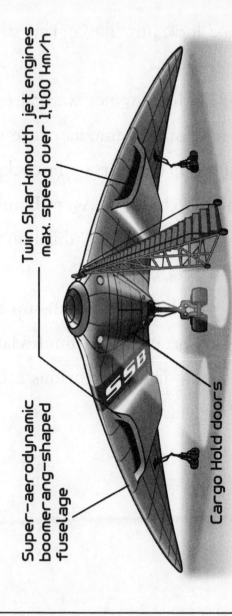

Super-aerodynamic boomerang-shaped fuselage

Twin Sharkmouth jet engines max. speed over 1,400 km/h

Cargo Hold doors

S.S.B. SuperSonic Boomerang Long-Distance Cargo Jet

And it *did* look just like a giant silver boomerang.

The jet's mighty engines were already howling, ready for an immediate take-off.

Zac sprinted up the stairs to the cockpit. He yelled hello to his pilot, Agent Bomber McGee. Bomber was usually third on the Spy Ladder.

Bomber gave him the thumbs-up and started take-off procedures. Minutes later, Zac was relaxing in the luxurious cabin, high above the ocean.

CHAPTER... ...FOUR

As the massive jet accelerated, Zac's SpyPad beeped. It was an email from Leon.

MISSION UPDATE: Reports just in claim the Prince disappeared while trekking on Yeti Mountain.

His royal guards were knocked out, so cannot report on what happened. A few of them claim they saw a yeti, but GIB scientists cannot confirm yetis even exist, so this seems unlikely.

Be careful!
– Agent Tech Head

EMAIL
>>> ON

The Hidden Kingdom was a few hours away. *I'd better enjoy GIB technology while I can!* thought Zac. *Snack time!*

He pressed a button on his seat console. A minute later, a sizzling hamburger with no tomato and extra sauce slid onto his seat tray.

Once Zac had finished his burger, he selected his SpyPad's new Sleep Learning function. Apparently, your brain can absorb facts while you snooze! Zac only wished he could use it for his school work.

Zac tilted his seat back, plugged in the HK info disc, and drifted off to sleep.

'Wakey, wakey, Agent Rock Star!'

Zac woke with a start to see Agent Bomber's grinning face.

'It's ten minutes to launch, Zac.'

Ten minutes? thought Zac, trying to clear his head. But good spies never looked flustered – especially not with spies *below* them on the Spy Ladder!

He glanced at his watch.

SPY CHRONOMETER
TIME: 3:59 AM & 52 SECONDS
MISSION TIME LEFT:
15 HOURS,
0 MINUTES
AND 8 SECONDS

'Ah, cool,' Zac said calmly. 'I'll just check my launch gear.'

Zac casually got up and walked out of the cabin, pulling on his backpack. Then he turned and sprinted towards the cargo bay.

Zac lifted a trapdoor and jumped down the stairs. Inside the hold was a massive hang-glider. A note taped to one of the wings read, *This craft has no landing gear. It's designed for mid-air connections.*

Zac strapped on the huge, transparent wings. *Flying over the mountains like a giant bug,* Zac grinned to himself. *Sounds fun!*

He slid into the bag hanging beneath the wings, and pulled on the helmet and oxygen mask.

Agent Bomber came down the stairs. Zac asked if he knew the connection details.

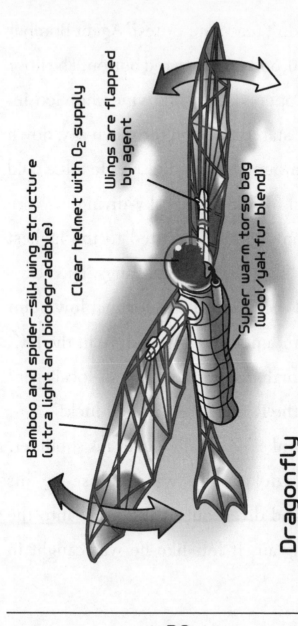

Bamboo and spider-silk wing structure
(ultra light and biodegradable)

Clear helmet with O₂ supply

Wings are flapped
by agent

Super warm torso bag
(wool/yak fur blend)

Dragonfly
High Altitude, Human-Powered, Air-to-Air Rendezvous Glider

'Didn't read your notes?' Agent Bomber grinned, and pressed a red button. The floor doors opened, and icy winds howled in.

Zac stared through the dawn sky, down at the mountains way below. He felt a cold thrill of fear. He loved sky-diving!

Agent Bomber pointed to the highest peaks. 'Those are the Ice Fangs. The HK is behind them. Head east for that low point in the mountains. Once you're in the HK, head north. You're meeting our local agent above the Royal Forest. Good luck!'

'Thanks!' Zac called over his shoulder.

He tucked the wings close to his body, and dived out of the plane into the freezing air. It felt like he was caught in a tornado. Zac was spiralling downwards, dangerously out of control!

Now, he thought to himself, *how do I fly this thing?* Then he remembered some GIB training he'd done in a similar flying suit.

He forced his wings away from his body and with a whoosh he stopped spinning and started flying.

Rules for flying human-powered gliders at 8000 metres

1. Flap hard
2. Stay high
3. Don't look down!

Soon he had the Dragonfly sailing toward the direction of the Ice Fangs. As he flapped his wings he felt like a big, awkward bird.

After an hour of flying, Zac's oxygen was running low. He was pleased to see the Ice Fangs towering before him.

Not far now! he thought. His arms and shoulders burned.

But Zac could feel the Dragonfly losing altitude. As he looked around, he realised ice was coating the wings. It was making the Dragonfly too heavy!

The mountains loomed up ahead as Zac continued to lose altitude. He forced his aching arms to keep flapping – he had to get over those mountains. But he was still heading straight for the wall of icy rock.

I'm going to crash into the mountain, thought Zac, gasping for air. *I need a plan!*

Zac could see black clouds approaching from his left. He knew a storm was coming. *I need a lift . . . and storm clouds often have strong updrafts!*

Zac shifted direction and flew straight into the storm cloud. He was suddenly surrounded by a thick grey mist. He couldn't see a metre in front of him!

Zac knew that if his plan failed, he would hit the mountain in seconds.

WHOOOOOOOOSHHH!

Suddenly, the Dragonfly was sucked up, like a leaf in a vacuum cleaner. Zac felt his stomach drop as he soared upwards, spinning dizzily. The roaring winds ripped at his wings.

Zac was blown out into clear air, passing just above the mountains.

Phew! I made it! grinned Zac, his heart still thumping in his chest.

He knew he had just missed the jagged mountain top by about 20 centimetres.

The Hidden Kingdom came into view, just as the sun was rising. Zac headed north, looking for the Royal Forest.

The storm cloud had ripped holes in the Dragonfly's delicate wings, and Zac was feeling exhausted. He started to shiver.

Zac locked his wings to 'glide' position and searched through his backpack.

It was still quite dark, and Zac had no idea how he was going to find and meet the local GIB agent.

He felt a small metal box in his bag. Zac opened it and white light blasted his eyes. Quickly shutting the box, Zac checked the label on the side.

SIGNAL LANTERN

Contains Solarite,
a naturally glowing mineral

Aiming the lantern north, Zac signalled 'A-G-E-N-T R-I-N-G-O'.

Just as Zac was wondering if a Hidden Kingdom agent would know Morse code, a faint light flashed up ahead.

It read 'A-G-E-N-T R-O-C-K S-T-A-R' in Morse code!

Zac glided towards the light. As he got closer, he saw a hot-air balloon up ahead. It was hovering above the forest. There was someone in the basket underneath, waving to him.

Riiiip!

But just then the Dragonfly's damaged wings tore wide open. Zac was so close, but he wasn't going to make it!

He unzipped his body cover and dived desperately towards the balloon's basket.

But Zac was too far away, and he plummeted towards the ground!

CHAPTER... ...FIVE

As Zac fell, he glimpsed a rope hanging under the balloon. He reached out for it, and . . . *Got it!* Zac jolted to a stop and, gripping the rope tightly, started to climb upwards.

A dark-haired young man helped him into the basket.

'Agent Rock Star,' Zac said, holding out his hand. 'You can call me Zac.'

'I am Agent Ringo,' grinned the youth. 'As in, Ringo Starr? I chose my name so I would be just like you. A rock star!'

Zac was confused. *Ringo Starr?* Wasn't

he one of the Beatles – that old band his grandpa used to listen to? When Zac thought about how remote the Hidden Kingdom was, it made sense that Ringo might like the same bands as his grandpa!

The local GIB agent handed him a steaming mug. Zac pulled off his oxygen mask, and took the mug gratefully.

'It's yak milk,' Ringo explained.

Zac hesitated, and then gulped down the

warm, creamy liquid. *Not bad,* he thought. *It's actually quite tasty.*

Ringo began talking about the mission. 'Most people believe the yeti took the Prince,' he said, shaking his head. 'But I do not. Next in line to the throne is Kah, the Prince's great uncle. Kah has been away for many years, but he mysteriously returned *very* soon after the kidnapping. He's saying the crown is now his.'

'Could he be the kidnapper?' Zac asked.

'I cannot prove it,' said Ringo. 'But Kah is cruel, and wants to change everything in our land. He will be a bad king.'

Zac's mind raced as he considered this new information. The words *white ninjas* suddenly popped into Zac's head.

Where did that thought come from? Zac wondered. Then he remembered the Sleep Learning he'd done on the flight. It was freaky to think Zac might know things he didn't even *know* he knew!

'SLEEP LEARNING' INFORMATION

Hidden Kingdom Cultures –
White Ninjas
Deadly Martial Artists
- Live on Yeti Mountain
- Fight with ice weapons
- Snow-white clothing
- Incredibly fast across snow

zzzZ z z z z z z z z z z z Z z z z z Z z z z z Z z z z z z z z z

Ringo started pulling on the anchor rope, and the balloon began descending gently towards the ground.

Zac was just going to ask Ringo about the white ninjas when he heard something whizzing towards them.

WHIZZ-SNAP!

Suddenly the balloon lurched violently as the anchor rope snapped in two. They were under attack! The two agents held on to the side of the balloon's basket.

WHIZZ-SNAP!

The balloon was hit again!

This time Zac was thrown sideways out of the basket. Zac tucked into a ball to soften the impact of his fall, but luckily they weren't too far from the ground. He hit the snow and rolled.

Looking up, he saw Ringo clinging to

the spinning basket as the balloon blew off into the mist. He was calling out to Zac. 'Find a white yak at the Golden Palace!'

Then Ringo was gone and Zac was alone on the slopes of the mountain.

He checked his watch.

SPY CHRONOMETER
TIME: 7:06 AM & 12 SECONDS
MISSION TIME LEFT:
11 HOURS,
53 MINUTES
AND 48 SECONDS

Zac's spy senses tingled as he heard a sound behind him. He ducked down.

WHIZZ-THUNK!

Zac spun around and saw an ice-disk that

had hissed past and buried itself deep in the tree trunk behind him. If Zac hadn't moved, it would have hit him right in the head!

Zac faked right, and then dived left for the cover of a thick tree trunk.

Zac knew he needed an escape route. Otherwise he wouldn't stand a chance in the snow against a white ninja! Thinking quickly, he dug his boots into the snow.

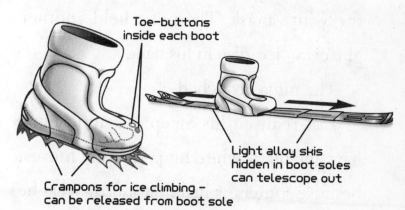

Toe-buttons inside each boot

Light alloy skis hidden in boot soles can telescope out

Crampons for ice climbing – can be released from boot sole

Tele-Ski Boots with Retractable Crampons

With his big toes, Zac pressed the buttons hidden inside his boots. He could feel the Tele-Skis shoot out the front of his boots — *underneath* the snow.

Just then a white shape cart-wheeled past Zac. The figure leapt into the air.

This guy's FAST, thought Zac. *And huge!*

The ninja landed in front of Zac. Two dark eyes glared at him through a slit in the white mask. The ninja held another glittering ice-disc in his hand.

The ninja crouched.

Zac realised his Sleep Learning must have included white ninja fighting moves, because somehow he knew *exactly* what he had to do.

The ninja raised his leg for a split-second before attacking. But Zac was ready. He kicked his Tele-Skis up out of the snow, and knocked the ninja onto his white butt!

Then Zac skied off down the slope, releasing Tele-Ski poles from his sleeves as he sped down the hill.

Looking over his shoulder, Zac saw the white ninja was up and following him. He looked like a whirling explosion of snow!

Zac was a great skier, but the ninja was gaining on him. He was moving across the snow at an incredible speed! Zac swerved wildly, dodging the ninja and ducking the ice-discs that whizzed through the air.

Up ahead, Zac could see a cliff looming. *Gulp!* He was heading straight for it! Zac's mind raced as he went through his options. But the ninja was right behind him, and it was too late to avoid the cliff.

If I have to ski jump, Zac thought, *I may as well try to break my personal best distance!*

With a deep breath, Zac skied right off the cliff!

CHAPTER... ...SIX

Zac tilted his body forward as he flew though the air — just like he had been taught in his GIB extreme skiing course.

Looking back over his shoulder, Zac saw that the ninja had stopped at the cliff's edge above him.

Zac could see the Hidden Kingdom far below — it looked amazing. *But now is not the time for sight-seeing,* he reminded himself.

He had a crash-landing to prepare for!

Zac let his Tele-Ski poles fall from his hands, and grabbed a pack of ParaGum from his pocket.

This ParaGum had better work! thought Zac, as he crammed

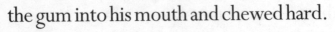

the gum into his mouth and chewed hard.

Zac pushed his tongue into the gum, and blew a bubble. The ground was getting closer and closer! Zac blew and blew, making the bubble bigger and bigger and . . .

WHOOF!

Zac's body jolted as he slowed to a drift.

The ParaGum was working!

Moments later, Zac splashed into a field and managed to perform a muddy commando roll. As the bubble dissolved into the mud, Zac set off towards the city. It looked about three kilometres away.

He hoped Ringo was OK, and had managed to land the balloon safely.

As Zac walked, he passed a few locals riding donkeys. He got a few funny looks, but no-one stopped him.

He was feeling uneasy, but couldn't put his finger on why.

Of course! he realised suddenly. With no cars, phones or music, it was eerily quiet in the Hidden Kingdom.

Zac studied the Golden Palace as he approached. It looked like a giant golden jewel box. It had five curved roofs, each roof smaller than the one below. Guards with sharp-looking bronze axes blocked the golden gates.

Zac watched from a distance as a tourist approached the guards. One of the guards tried to speak to the tourist in English.

'Lucky Starbuck?' the guard asked, in a very strong accent.

The tourist looked confused, and was turned away.

Zac knew who Lucky Starbuck was! He was the mop-haired star of the show *Lucky's World*. Lucky travelled the world, showing off and interviewing famous people.

Someone is expecting Lucky, Zac realised, as an idea started to form. *He must be coming to interview Kah!*

Zac was busting to get on with the mission, but he knew he should find Ringo first. Zac remembered Ringo's last words – something about finding a white yak.

Zac soon spotted a white cow-like thing under a tree, not far from the gates. Zac didn't really know what a yak looked like, but he decided to check it out.

As he got closer, Zac was sure he heard it whispering, 'Zac Power! Follow, please!'

For a moment, Zac thought he was going crazy. *Maybe I hit my head when I fell?*

he thought, rubbing his temples.

Then he realised it was actually Agent Ringo, in a yak suit!

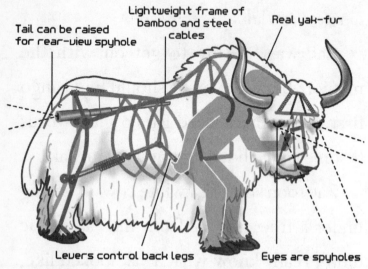

Lightweight frame of bamboo and steel cables

Real yak-fur

Tail can be raised for rear-view spyhole

Levers control back legs

Eyes are spyholes

Mobile Yak Suit (GIB – Hidden Kingdom Branch)

Zac followed Ringo at a distance. They reached a small, round hut with a pointy thatched roof, and went inside.

Agent Ringo struggled out of his

disguise, grinning. He explained that he had dropped safely from the balloon into the Royal Forest, and hiked back.

Zac told Ringo about his encounter with the very scary white ninja.

'Attacked by a white ninja!' said Ringo, amazed. 'They normally keep to themselves.'

Zac checked his watch.

SPY CHRONOMETER
TIME: 9:40 AM & 6 SECONDS
MISSION TIME LEFT:
9 HOURS,
19 MINUTES
AND 54 SECONDS

'The clock's ticking! I am going to sneak into the palace,' said Zac, picking up his backpack and getting ready to set off. 'I need to know if Kah is involved.'

'You'll never get into the palace without an appointment!' cried Ringo.

'I have one!' Zac said, winking at the confused agent.

The royal guards stared in shock as a boy rode up to the palace gates on the back of a white yak.

'Whoa, Snowball!' called the boy in a loud voice. 'I'm Lucky Starbuck! Kah is waiting for me, dudes! Open sesame!'

The guards immediately lowered their axes and opened the gates. The boy and his yak started walking up the impressive flight of golden steps.

'Too heavy!' the yak complained in a muffled voice.

Zac checked that no-one was watching, and then jumped off. Ringo went off to explore the palace and Zac marched through a huge golden entrance.

'Your majesty! Interview time!' called Zac in his most annoying Lucky Starbuck voice.

He hoped Kah hadn't seen too many episodes of *Lucky's World*. Zac knew his yak-hair wig looked pretty fake.

A hooded white figure led Zac into a huge room draped with colourful fabric and lamps. A fat man lounged on cushions, being fed grapes and chocolates by servants.

He stared coldly at Zac. 'Mr Starbuck!' Kah rumbled. 'I thought you were older.'

'Ah, the camera adds on *years*, your highness!' Zac laughed.

Kah didn't look convinced. Zac decided to get on with the interview before Kah threw him out of the palace.

'Now,' said Zac, pretending to look at a list of questions. 'The Prince has been kidnapped, I hear. Where did this happen?'

'Kidnapped?' roared Kah. 'No! Yetis took the Prince! It was near the Blue C – ' Kah stopped himself suddenly. 'It was not a *kidnapping*!' He spluttered, and threw down his chocolate. 'GUARDS!'

'Apologies, your highness,' Zac said quickly. He needed more time! 'It is so *noble* of you to accept the crown!' Zac added.

Kah seemed pleased enough by this comment to have another chocolate.

Zac decided to keep up with the flattery. 'What will you be wearing at the crowning tonight, your highness? Any hints?'

'Well,' Kah said, patting his huge belly, 'the traditional royal robes won't fit my, err, *manly* frame. So I shall change tradition, and wear *white* robes!' He smirked.

'WOW!' gushed Zac. 'New king, new ideas! I bet you have some great plans?'

Kah was enjoying himself. 'Yes,' he nodded. 'I will modernise my country. My lazy people will work.' Then Kah broke off. 'Enough! I will reveal all when I am King.' He looked suspiciously at Zac. 'Your hair looks . . . *strange*, Mr Starbuck.'

Kah signalled to a guard standing nearby.

The guard moved towards Zac.

Zac jumped back, screaming, 'Don't touch the hair! Don't you know I'm on the cover of *Hair Affair* magazine this month?'

Zac turned on his heel and stomped out of the palace. He wasn't sure if his tantrum had convinced Kah he was Lucky Starbuck, but he didn't plan on waiting to find out!

Outside the gates, Zac saw the *real* Lucky arrive in an armchair carried by assistants. Lucky was screaming, 'Where is my hair brush?'

Zac grinned as he headed back to meet Agent Ringo.

CHAPTER... ...SEVEN

Ringo returned to the hut soon after Zac. He jumped out of the suit, looking upset.

'I overheard Kah's guards talking about their master's plans. It is awful! Once he is King, Kah will *melt down* the Golden Palace . . . and *sell* it! And Kah wants to flood the Kingdom to make a huge artificial lake – '

'A lake?' Zac asked, puzzled. 'Why would Kah want to build a huge lake? Did the guards say anything about that?'

'Yes! Kah is going to build lakeside mansions – to sell to the world's richest buyers! We local people will be *homeless*. We will be Kah's *slave labour*.'

'Well, I may know where the Prince is,' said Zac. 'Kah let something slip in the interview. He said the kidnapping happened near the Blue C – but then he stopped himself. Any ideas?'

Ringo thought for a moment. 'I know!' he cried. 'Maybe he was talking about the Blue Caves! They are high on Yeti Mountain. It's a long, deadly climb!'

Zac wasn't so worried about this. He was a very good spy and an experienced rock-climber, after all. 'Well, I'd better get climbing!' he said, pulling off his yak-hair wig.

'Err . . . yes . . . me too!' Ringo muttered nervously, as he followed Zac.

Zac wasn't sure he wanted another spy on his heels – he was used to spying solo! But he could hardly say that to Ringo. So together they set off for Yeti Mountain.

They kept to wooded paths to avoid being spotted. Soon Zac could see Yeti Mountain looming up ahead. Zac had to admit it *did* look really difficult to climb.

As they neared the Royal Forest, Zac's spy senses tingled. He gave the GIB *stop* hand-signal, and crouched down. He pulled on his white hood and looked around.

But Ringo completely missed Zac's signal, and strolled into the forest clearing. He was whistling loudly!

Has this guy done any GIB training? Zac wondered.

Snowballs sped through the air, hitting Ringo's temples at high speed. They were so perfectly aimed, they knocked him out!

Deadly speed and accuracy? thought Zac. *This must be the work of white ninjas!*

Zac dropped to the ground as three ninjas leapt down silently from the trees. He lay still and hoped his all-white suit would blend into the snow! Sure enough, the ninjas ran right past him, and tied Ringo's wrists behind his back.

'No visitors for the Prince, after all!' joked one of the ninjas.

So the white ninjas do *have the Prince!* Zac thought. *I'm on the right track!*

He looked at his watch.

SPY CHRONOMETER
TIME: 12:15 PM & 6 SECONDS
MISSION TIME LEFT:
6 HOURS,
44 MINUTES
AND 54 SECONDS

Zac wanted to help his fellow agent, but he was sure the ninjas wouldn't hurt Ringo. Plus, rescuing him would almost certainly mean failing the mission.

Zac had to keep going. After a half-hour's running, Zac had reached the snowline. He was sweating, but there was no time to rest. He climbed higher and higher.

As the hours dragged past, the ice became incredibly steep and slippery. Zac released his Ice Claws — now he could even climb *vertical* ice!

Zac fought to catch his breath. His leg muscles were burning.

The climb was taking longer than Zac had expected. He was very fit, but this was crazy! He could see the mountain's peak up ahead, but it was still far above him

whUmP
whUmP
wHUMP!

Zac dropped to a ledge of snow as a helicopter passed high overhead.

Hey, helicopters are illegal here! thought Zac. *That could be Kah,* he realised, *heading for the Blue Caves the easy way!*

After two more hours of climbing, Zac could hardly feel his fingers and toes. The weather was getting worse and worse.

Soon a snowstorm blew in, pushing Zac against the side of the mountain. He was lost in whiteness! Even Zac's excellent sense of direction couldn't help him out this time.

Feeling dizzy and numb, Zac knew he needed a helping hand.

My Glookifruit energy chews! he thought vaguely, as he tried to grab them from his backpack. *Too numb . . . so tired . . . must . . . stay . . . awake . . .*

But before Zac could find his energy chews, he fell to the snow, unconscious.

CHAPTER... ...EIGHT

Zac dreamt he was being carried by a big white bear. It was all warm and fluffy.

Some time later Zac woke up with a start. He looked around and saw he was inside an ice cave. He was lying next to a crackling campfire.

Where am I? Zac wondered. *And was that bear a dream? Who rescued me?*

He was alone, but an enormous stone

bowl of soup sat steaming on the cave floor nearby. It smelt good!

Zac drank the hot, salty soup gratefully. He didn't want to know what was in it. *Yak-hoof soup?* he wondered, pulling a face.

For dessert, Zac gobbled some high-energy Glookifruit chews.

Glookifruit
High-Energy Chews

With his strength returning, Zac jumped up to explore the ice cave.

He noticed some huge footprints in the snow leading out of the cave. They looked like human footprints, but each one was about 45 centimetres long!

A yeti? The abominable snowman? Zac puzzled. He shook his head and laughed at himself. *Nah, they're not real!*

He took a moment to look at his grandpa's watch and gasped. He only had three hours before Kah would be crowned as king!

SPY CHRONOMETER
TIME: 4:01 PM & 49 SECONDS
MISSION TIME LEFT:
2 HOURS,
58 MINUTES
AND 11 SECONDS

Zac walked quickly to the edge of the cave towards the patch of sky, and then stopped suddenly. The cave opened out onto a vertical cliff! One more step and he would have fallen thousands of metres!

He edged away from the cliff. Walking back into the cave, Zac found an icy tunnel leading into the mountain.

I guess this is the only way to go, thought Zac, as he set off down the tunnel. He was still thinking about those huge footprints.

As he got further into the mountain, it became too dark to see. Zac reached into his backpack and opened his Solarite lantern. The tunnel's walls glowed blue. *Are these the Blue Caves?* wondered Zac.

Up ahead, Zac could see that the tunnel split into two. Should he go left, or right?

Zac stepped into the left tunnel. The air was still, and smelled stale. He tried the right tunnel instead. Zac felt a tiny breeze, and the air was fresher.

Zac decided to leave a trail of Glookifruit chews to mark his route — just in case he got lost and had to return along the tunnel.

He headed off down the right tunnel, dropping a Glookifruit every few minutes.

Hansel and Gretel style! smiled Zac to himself.

Twenty minutes — and many Glookifruits — later, Zac saw a faint light ahead. He tip-toed towards it.

The light was coming from a crack in the tunnel wall.

Through the gap, Zac could see down into a huge ice cavern. A fat man surrounded by white ninjas was laughing at a dark-haired boy.

Zac recognised the big guy — it was Kah! Zac peered at the boy. *That must be the Prince!* he thought.

Zac wondered how he was going to rescue the Prince. There were loads of white ninjas standing guard.

How would Zac get past them all?

He heard a low growl behind him, and turned to see a white fox-like creature with sharp teeth standing there. It had a bushy, black-tipped tail, and was chewing one of Zac's Glookifruits!

An Snow Fox! thought Zac, as the information sprang into his mind. *Thanks again, Sleep Learning!*

The white fox snarled at him, as if demanding more Glookifruits.

'How far will you go for a Glookifruit?' Zac whispered to the fox.

He checked his pocket. He only had two left! Zac squeezed slowly through the crack, and onto a thin ledge above the cavern. The white fox watched keenly.

Zac showed the fox the pink Glookifruit. Its pale eyes locked onto the lolly.

Zac took a deep breath and threw the Glookifruit into the cavern, towards Kah. It sailed down and dropped right into Kah's broad leather boot! *Bull's eye!*

The fox took off like a furry torpedo after the lolly. It attacked Kah's boots, sharp teeth bared. Chaos erupted as Kah bellowed and kicked out at the fox! Ninjas rushed to help him.

Fox attack — the perfect distraction!

CHAPTER...
...NINE

While no-one was looking, Zac quickly slid down the icy wall into the cavern.

He felt around in his backpack and pulled out what looked like a salt-shaker. Zac held it above his head and shook it. A fine black dust floated down, and Zac saw the light dim around him.

A second later, two ninjas marched right past Zac. They couldn't see him! There was just a patch of shadow where Zac stood.

Shadow Dust really works! Zac thought, making a mental note to thank Leon next time he saw him.

Zac's shadowy shape moved slowly towards the Prince. Now that Zac was close, the Prince could just see him. The Prince winked.

Cool guy, thought Zac. *Now to rescue him …*

Kah was still struggling with the fox, which had its nose down the wrong boot. The guards finally pulled the fox away.

Kah suddenly looked up and pointed at the Prince. He barked a command.

Zac froze. Had he been seen? He moved

back slowly. Two ninjas hurried towards him
. . . and bent to lift the Prince.

They still haven't seen me!

The ninjas dragged the Prince off down
a tunnel. Kah stuck close to them, still
looking nervous about fox attacks. Zac
followed at a distance down the tunnel.

Zac heard a noise up ahead and quickly
flattened himself against the tunnel wall.
Kah and his ninjas hurried back past
without the Prince.

Once they were out of sight, Zac ran
down the tunnel to find the Prince.

BOOOOM! BOOM CRASH!

Loud booms echoed through the walls.
Looking around, Zac saw that the ninjas

were smashing down the timber supports at the tunnel's entrance! Massive chunks of ice crashed to the ground. And suddenly Zac was in total darkness.

They had deliberately collapsed the entrance! Zac and the Prince were trapped in the freezing dark. Zac dug out his Solarite lantern again, and opened it.

'Who's there?' called the Prince.

Zac hurried down the tunnel and found the Prince tied up on the floor.

'Zac Power, your majesty,' said Zac politely, cutting the Prince's ropes with his Ice Claws. 'GIB secret agent. I'm here to get you to the ceremony!'

'Thank you, Zac Power!' the Prince

said, rubbing his wrists.

Don't thank me yet, Zac thought to himself, *we still have to get out of here.*

'Kah has been planning this for years,' the Prince explained. 'He flies in and out of the Hidden Kingdom in an illegal helicopter. He promised the white ninjas riches and power if they help him.'

Zac looked at his grandpa's watch.

SPY CHRONOMETER
TIME: 6:00 PM & 2 SECONDS
MISSION TIME LEFT:
0 HOURS,
59 MINUTES
AND 58 SECONDS

There was just one hour until the ceremony! Kah was going to become King!

Zac noticed a white shape further down the tunnel. *It's that greedy fox!*

'Let's follow the fox, your majesty,' said Zac, helping the Prince to stand up.

The two boys hurried after the fox. It darted along the icy maze, stopping to sniff the floor before choosing a direction.

At last the fox led them into the sunlight, out on a high rocky ledge. They stood on a thin, snow-covered shelf, on the side of the mountain.

The fox was staring hungrily at Zac's pockets. Zac reached in and found his last Glookifruit. He threw it to the fox. The fox snapped up the lolly and darted back into the tunnel.

Looking down from the cliff, Zac could see the Golden Palace, sparkling in the setting sun. But they were still 2000 metres above it, and the crowning ceremony was starting in just ten minutes!

Zac squatted down to look through his backpack. *No more ParaGum left. Only one set of skis . . .* Zac was out of ideas. How on earth was he going to get the Prince down the mountain in just a few minutes?

FLAP . . . FLAP FLAP FLAP . . .

And what is that annoying noise? Zac wondered, looking around.

CHAPTER... ...TEN

Zac jumped up and edged carefully along the narrow ledge, trying not to look down. High up on the rock face, Zac saw a rope flapping in the wind.

Zac laughed in surprise. It was Ringo's hot-air balloon! He freed the rope and tied a knot at its end.

'Your majesty, this is our only chance,' called Zac to the Prince. 'Hold the rope between your knees, and keep your feet on the knot.'

The Prince swallowed nervously before grabbing the rope. Zac grabbed the rope as well, and together they jumped off the cliff. The balloon began to sink steadily. The wind blew them away from the mountain.

Zac watched as they got closer and closer to the palace. There was only four minutes to the ceremony. *Will we make it?*

Zac and the Prince were just 200 metres above the Golden Palace when suddenly ice-discs started whizzing past.

WHIZZ-SNAP!

The white ninjas must have spotted them!

A disc ripped a hole in the balloon, sending it rushing towards the ground.

Zac tried to think through the options. *The balloon still has some air in it. If its load was lighter, it might get the Prince down safely.*

'Hold on, your highness!' yelled Zac, as he let go. He plummeted down towards the Golden Palace. Then, as Zac hit the curved roof, he clicked his Tele-Skis out, and skied down the steep tiles. The curved edges flipped him up into the night air, sending Zac flying towards the branches of a tree overlooking the palace courtyard.

Zac could see Kah in the courtyard below, dressed in white robes and surrounded by ninjas. The royal crown rested on a pillow. The ceremony was about to start!

Zac had to make a distraction. Quickly he called out, wanting to stop to the crowning until the Prince got there. 'ECNIRP SI EREH!' he yelled, in Hidden Kingdomese, meaning, *The Prince is here*.

The crowd rushed forward, cheering, as the Prince's deflating balloon landed safely in the palace courtyard. The Prince stood proudly, and pointed at the stunned Kah. 'Arrest this kidnapper!'

The royal guards moved quickly to seize Kah and his ninjas.

Courtiers surrounded the Prince, so Zac couldn't see him for a moment. When they moved away, Zac saw the Prince was wearing the royal robes. He looked up at Zac and winked.

The crowd roared as the Prince entered the palace to be crowned.

Zac climbed down from the tree as Kah and his ninjas were led away in chains.

Zac told the royal guards about Agent Ringo. The guards then questioned the scowling Kah, who told them where Ringo was being held. Zac knew his fellow agent would be OK.

Then the royal guards led Zac in to meet the new King.

'Thank you, Zac Power. I owe you my life,' said the newly crowned King. 'You shall receive whatever reward you wish!'

Zac's mind raced. *My own personal white ninja? A luxury hot-air balloon with butler?*

But Zac knew GIB spies couldn't accept gifts. And he also knew his dad was waiting for him to get home so they could go and have dinner at his granny's.

'I only want to go home, your highness,' Zac said, bowing politely.

The King smiled and led Zac into his private rooms. The King pulled back a rug, revealing a hidden trap door.

'The royal escape chute!' said the King. 'It's normally for royal bottoms only,' he grinned.

The King handed Zac some really ugly leather shorts. *What do I need these for?* Zac wondered as pulled them on over his climbing suit.

'The escape chute ends at the Hidden Kingdom's border. I think you will find that it is, as you would say . . . *sick fun!*' smiled the King.

They shook hands, and Zac jumped into the chute. It took a few seconds to speed up, but soon Zac was hurtling around corners and cork-screwing past rock fossils.

So this is what the special pants are for! Zac thought, as smoke started pouring off the leather shorts. It was better than any theme-park ride, and it went for ages!

Finally, Zac shot out of the tunnel into the sunshine. He landed with a splash in an icy river, putting out his smoking pants.

Mission complete! And he had done it without any high-tech gadgets!

But now that he was out of the Hidden Kingdom, it was tech time!

Zac chuckled as he pulled his SpyPad out from his backpack. He sent off a message to GIB headquarters.

CLASSIFIED

Requesting immediate pick-up. Mission successful. Suffering extreme technology withdrawal and hat-hair (please send large tube of super-strength hair gel).

— AGENT ROCK STAR

EMAIL
>>> ON

Then Zac got out his iPod and settled back to one of Axe Grinder's loudest hits.

Hmmm, I wonder what granny is making for dinner …

… **THE END** …

MISSION CHECKLIST
How many have you read?

POISON ISLAND 1

DEEP WATERS 2

MIND GAMES 3

FROZEN FEAR 4

TOMB OF DOOM 5

NIGHT RAID 6

LUNAR STRIKE 7

SUDDEN DROP 8

BLOCKBUSTER 9

SHOCKWAVE 10

HIGH RISK 11

UNDERCOVER 12

SKY HIGH 13

VOLCANIC PANIC 14

BOOT CAMP 15

SWAMP RACE 16

HORROR HOUSE 17

THRILL RIDE 18

CLOSE SHAVE 19

SHIPWRECK 2